The Ant
and the
Grasshopper

Retold by Diane Marwood

Illustrated by Gabriele Antonini

Crabtree Publishing Company

www.crabtreebooks.com

Crabtree Publishing Company
www.crabtreebooks.com
1-800-387-7650

PMB 59051, 350 Fifth Ave.   616 Welland Ave.
59th Floor,   St. Catharines, ON
New York, NY 10118   L2M 5V6

Published by Crabtree Publishing in 2012
Printed in the U.S.A./052012/FA20120413

Series editor: Jackie Hamley
Editor: Kathy Middleton
Proofreader: Reagan Miller
Series advisor: Dr. Hilary Minns
Series designer: Peter Scoulding
Print and Production coordinator:
  Katherine Berti

Text © Franklin Watts 2009
Illustration © Gabriele Antonini 2009

The rights of Diane Marwood
to be identified as the author
and Gabriele Antonini as the
illustrator of this Work have
been asserted.

First published in 2009
by Franklin Watts
(A division of Hachette
Children's Books)

Library and Archives Canada
Cataloguing in Publication

Marwood, Diane
    The ant and the grasshopper / retold by
Diane Marwood ; illustrated by Gabriele Antonini.

(Tadpoles: tales)
Issued also in electronic format.
ISBN 978-0-7787-7889-9 (bound).--
ISBN 978-0-7787-7901-8 (pbk.)

    1. Ants--Juvenile literature. 2. Grasshoppers--
Juvenile literature. I. Antonini, Gabriele II. Title.
III. Series: Tadpoles (St. Catharines, Ont.). Tales

PZ8.2.M37An 2012   j398.24'525796   C2012-902479-1

Library of Congress
Cataloging-in-Publication Data

CIP available at Library of Congress

This kind of story is called a fable. It was written by a Greek author called Aesop over 2,500 years ago. Fables are stories that can teach something. Can you figure out what the lesson in this fable is?

One day, Grasshopper was laying in the hot sun, just singing.

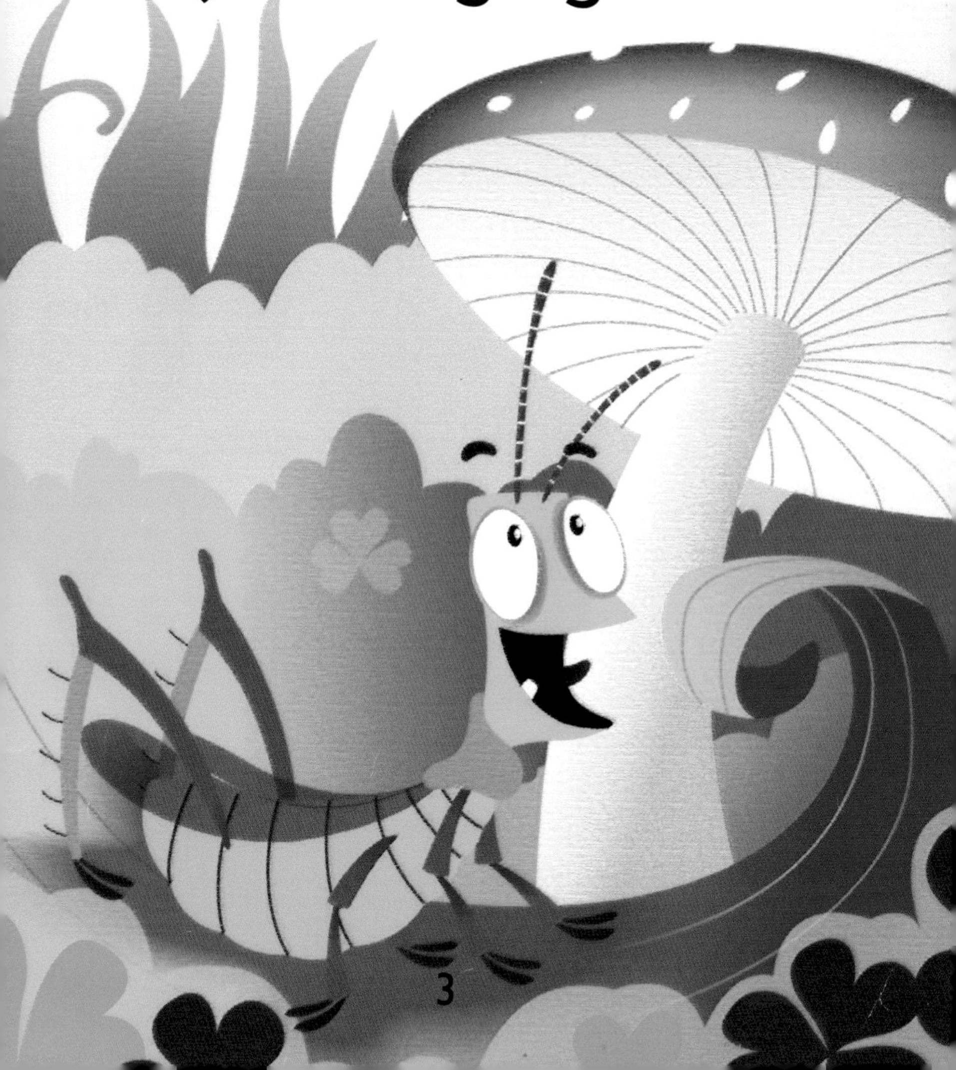

The ants were busy finding grain to store for winter.

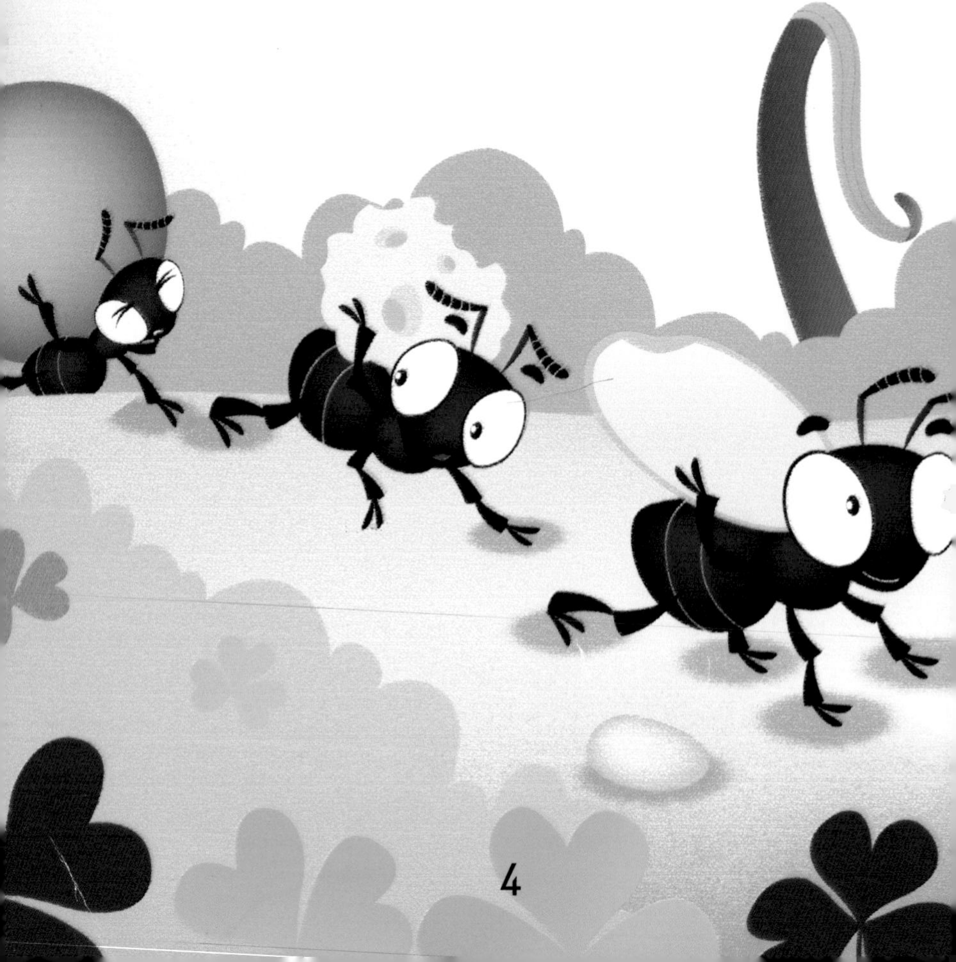

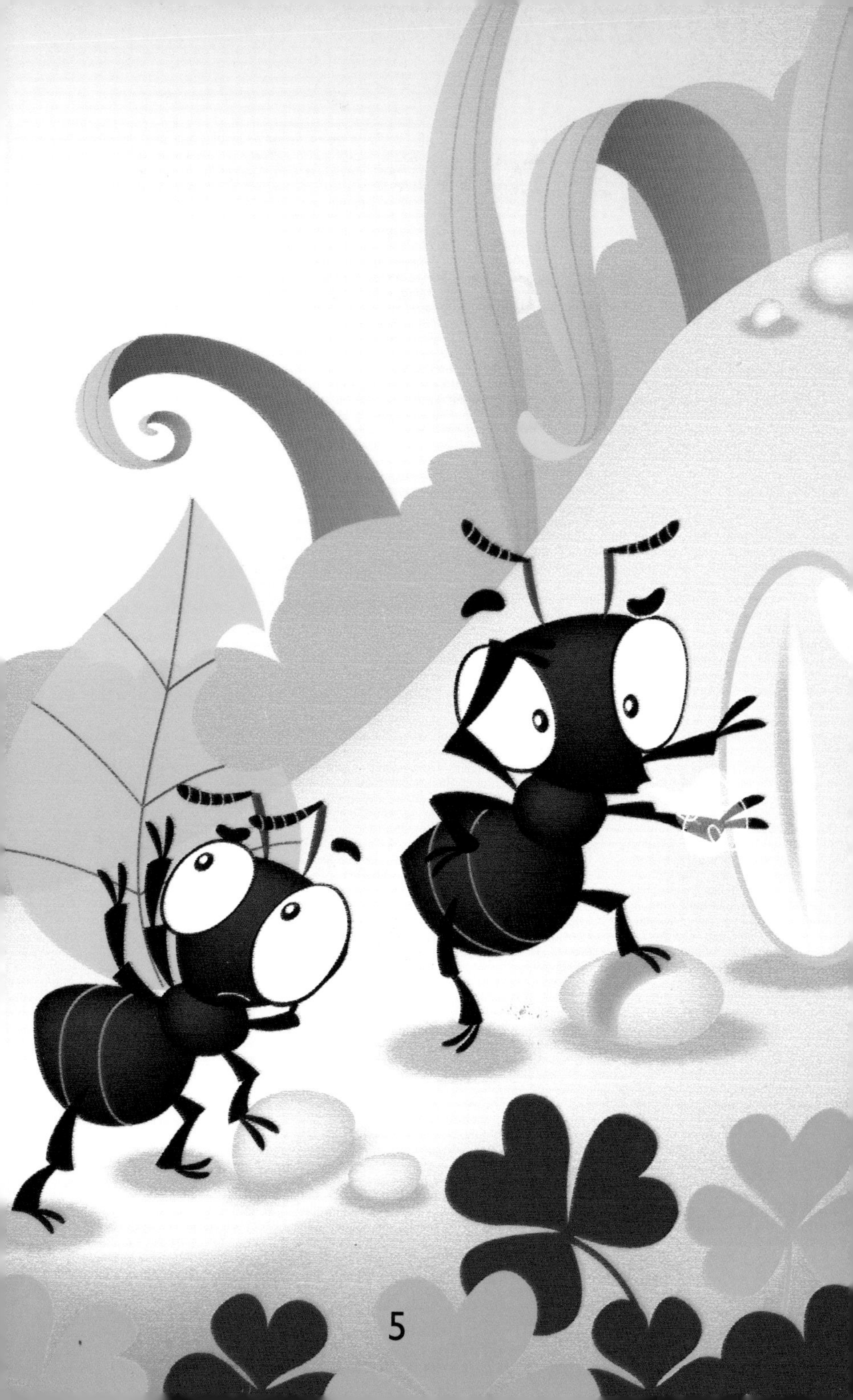

"Slow down, Ant.
It is too hot to work!"
called Grasshopper.

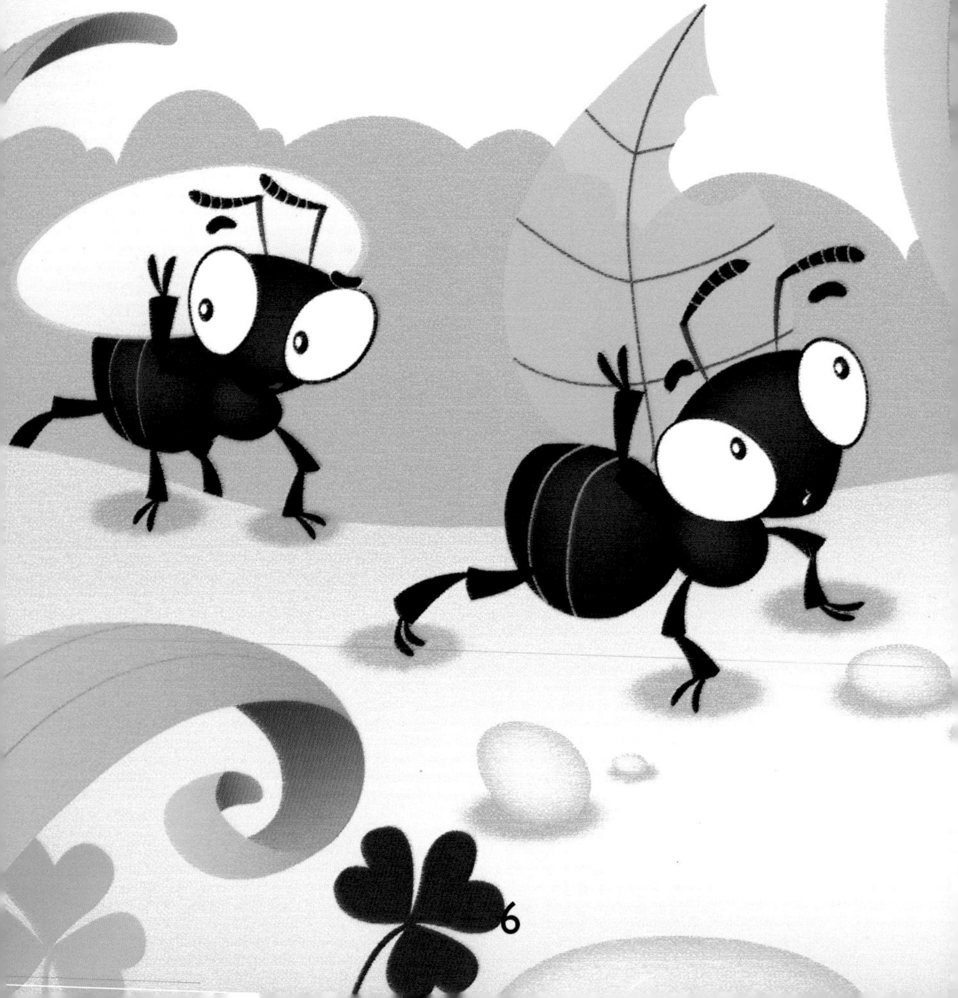

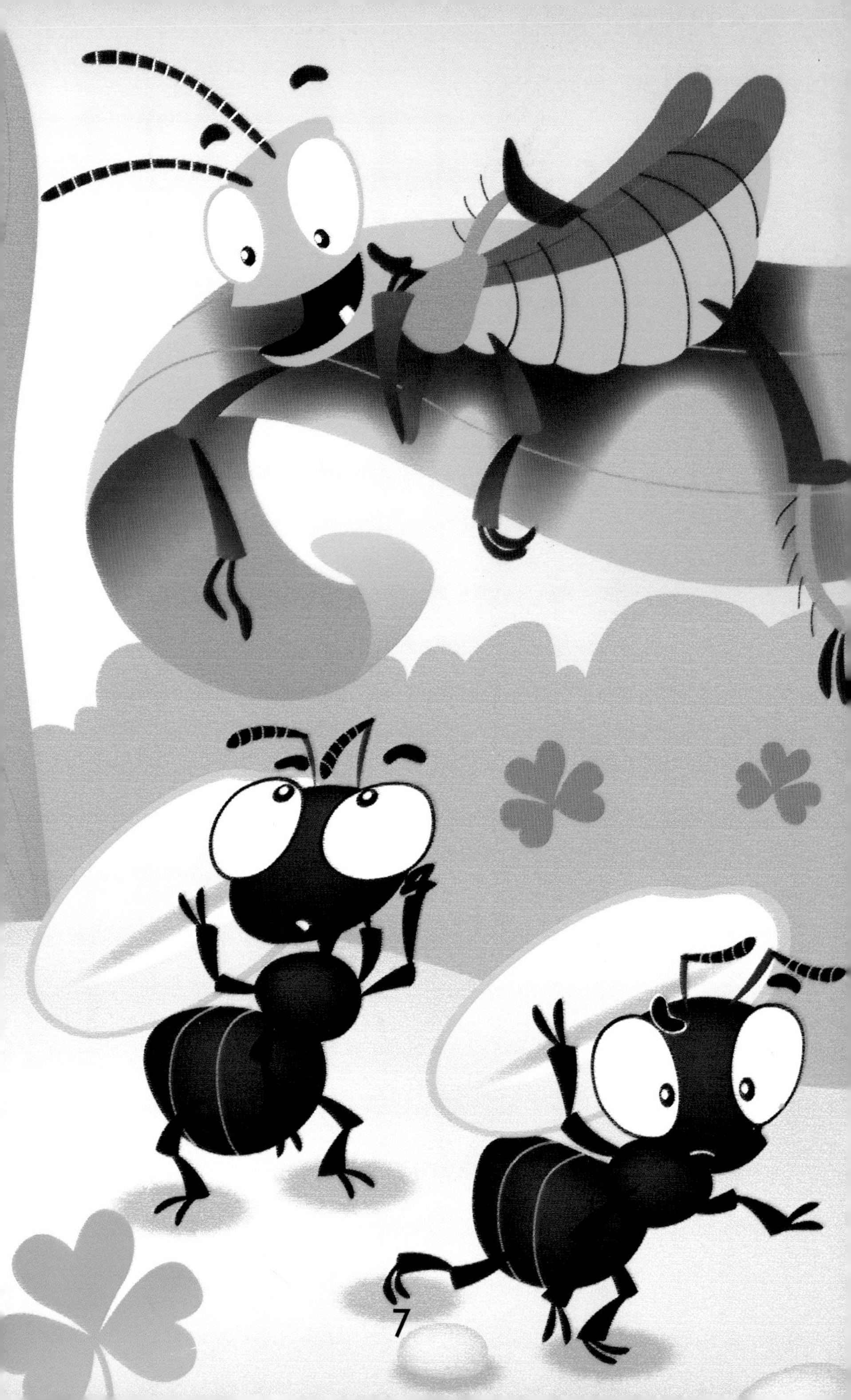

"You should be finding grain for winter, too!" Ant called back.

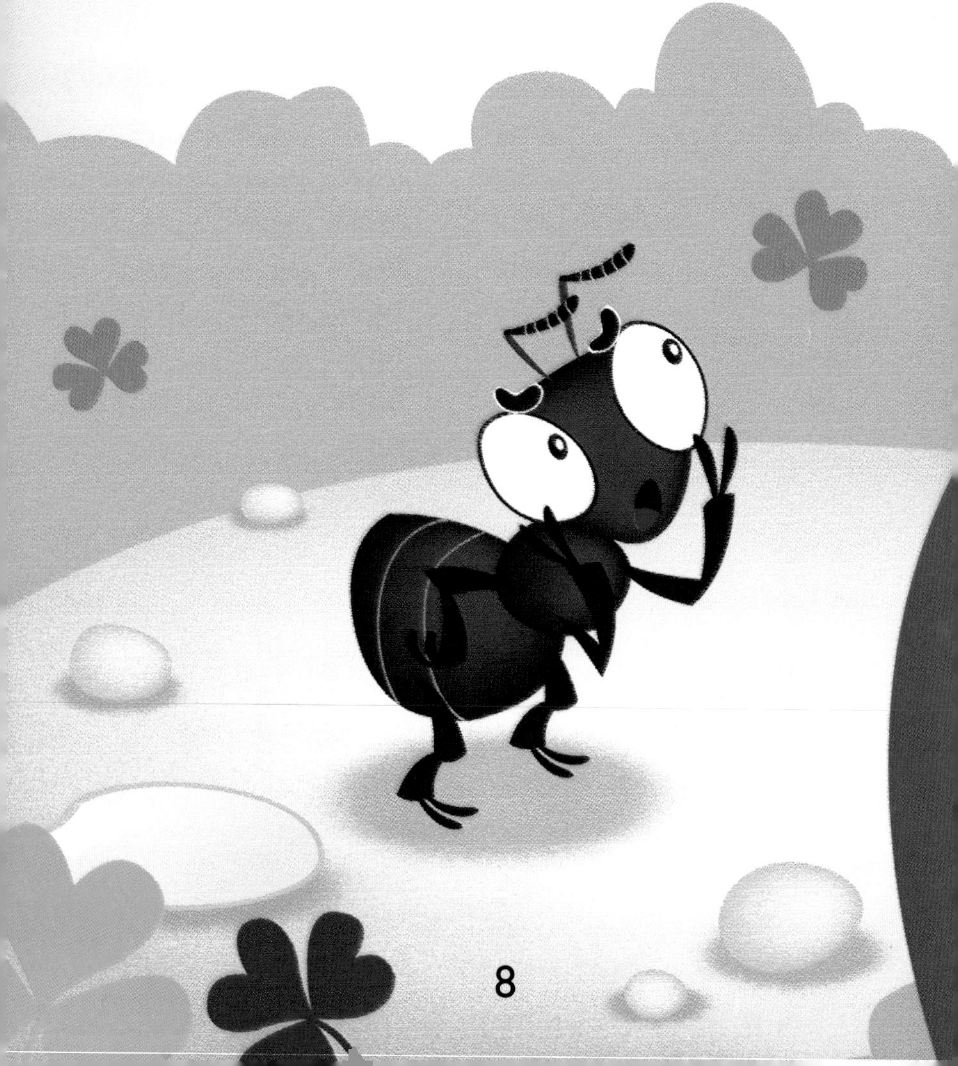

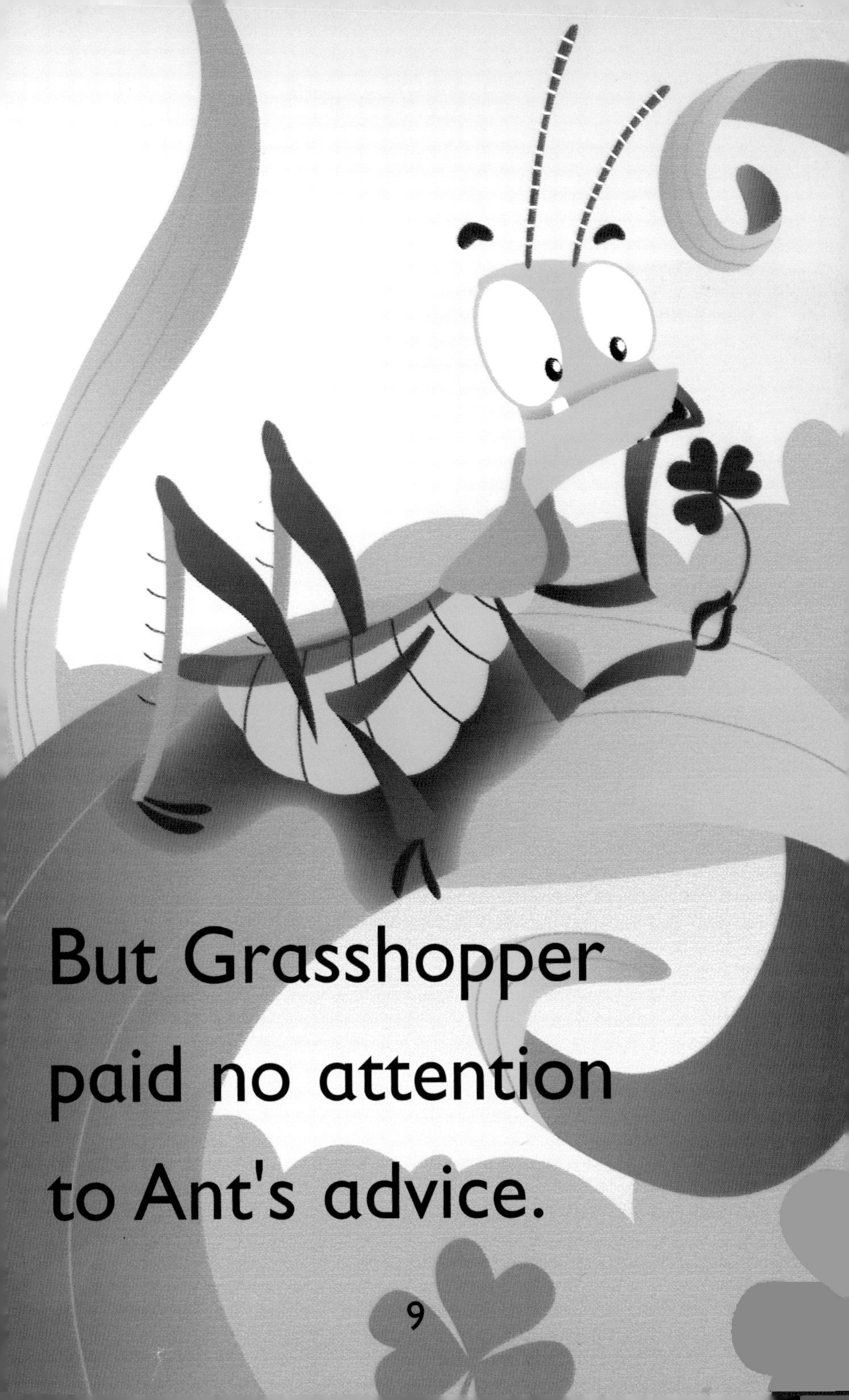

But Grasshopper paid no attention to Ant's advice.

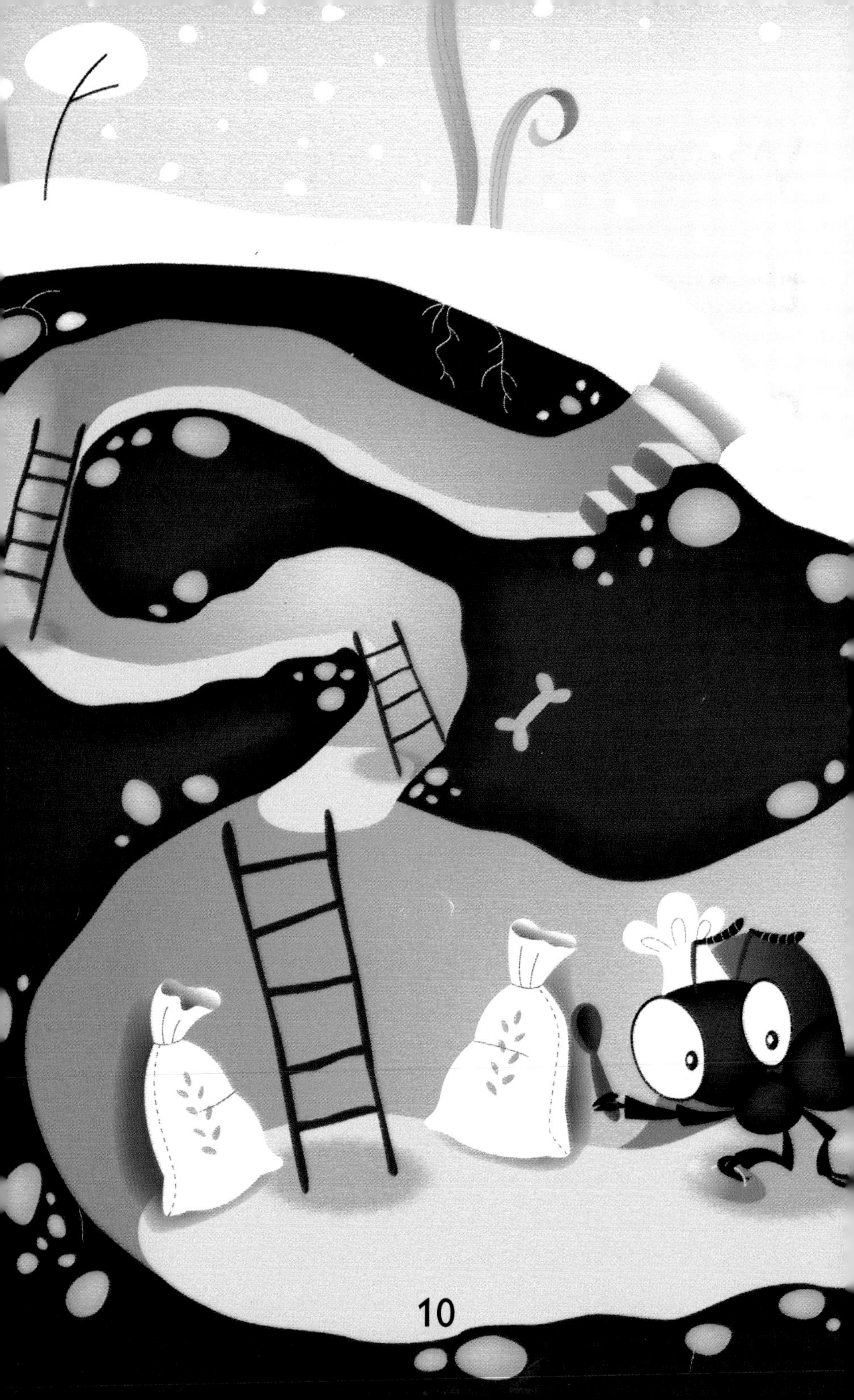

When cold winter came,
the ants kept warm
and ate their grain.

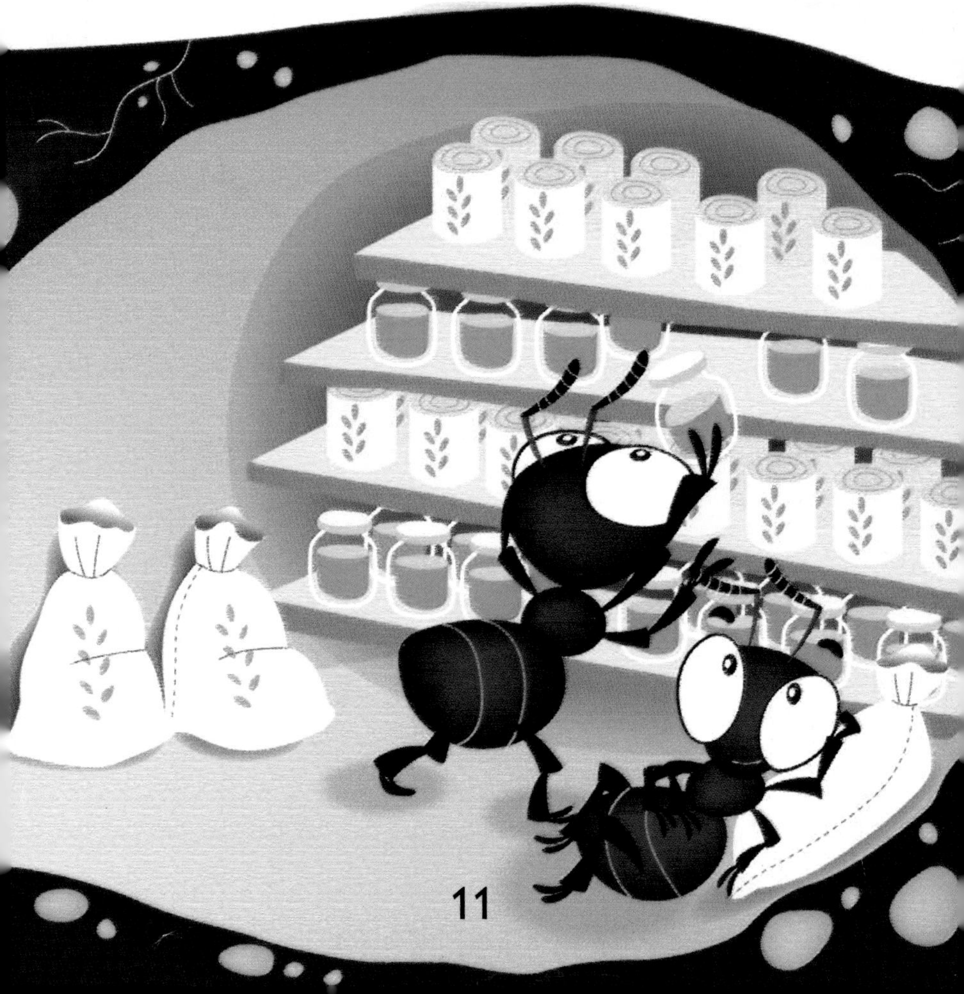

One cold morning, the ants saw Grasshopper.

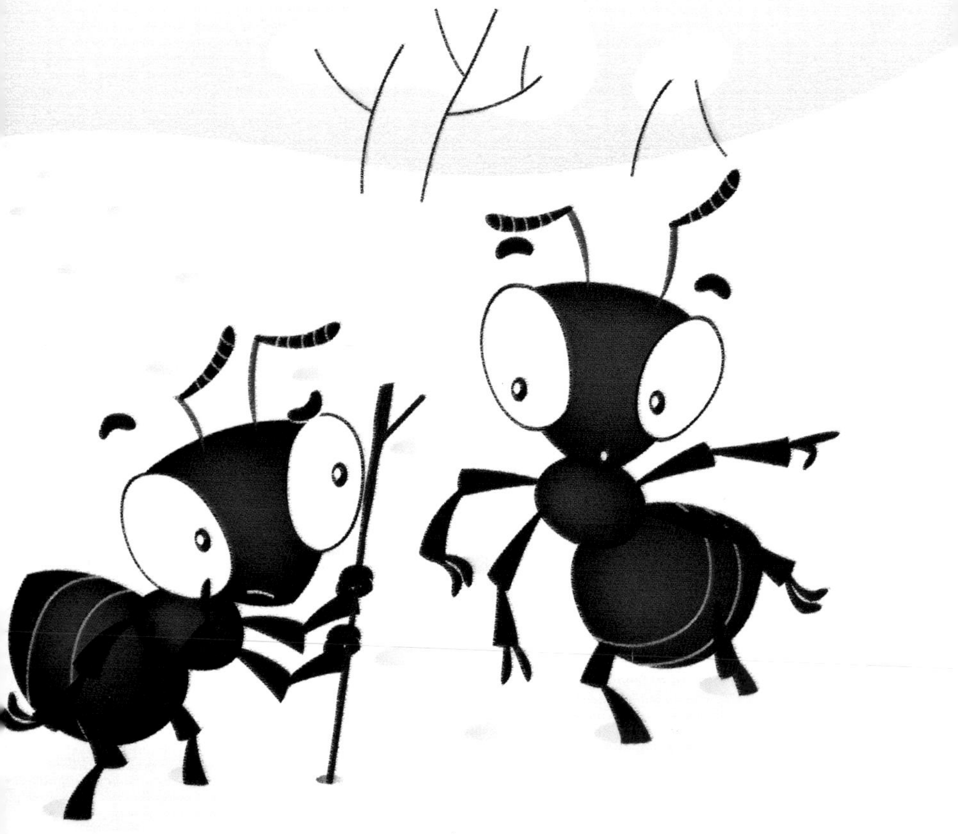

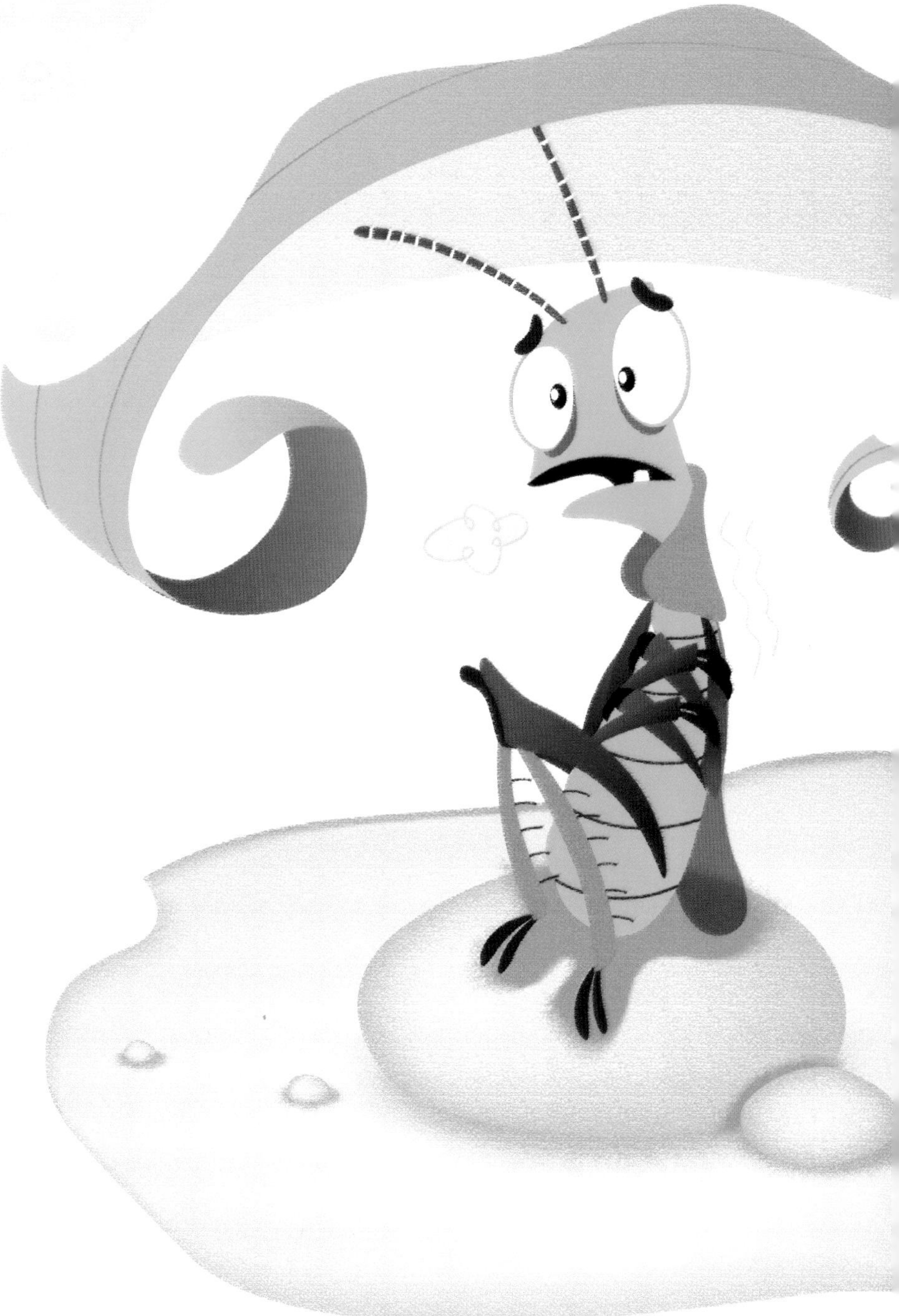

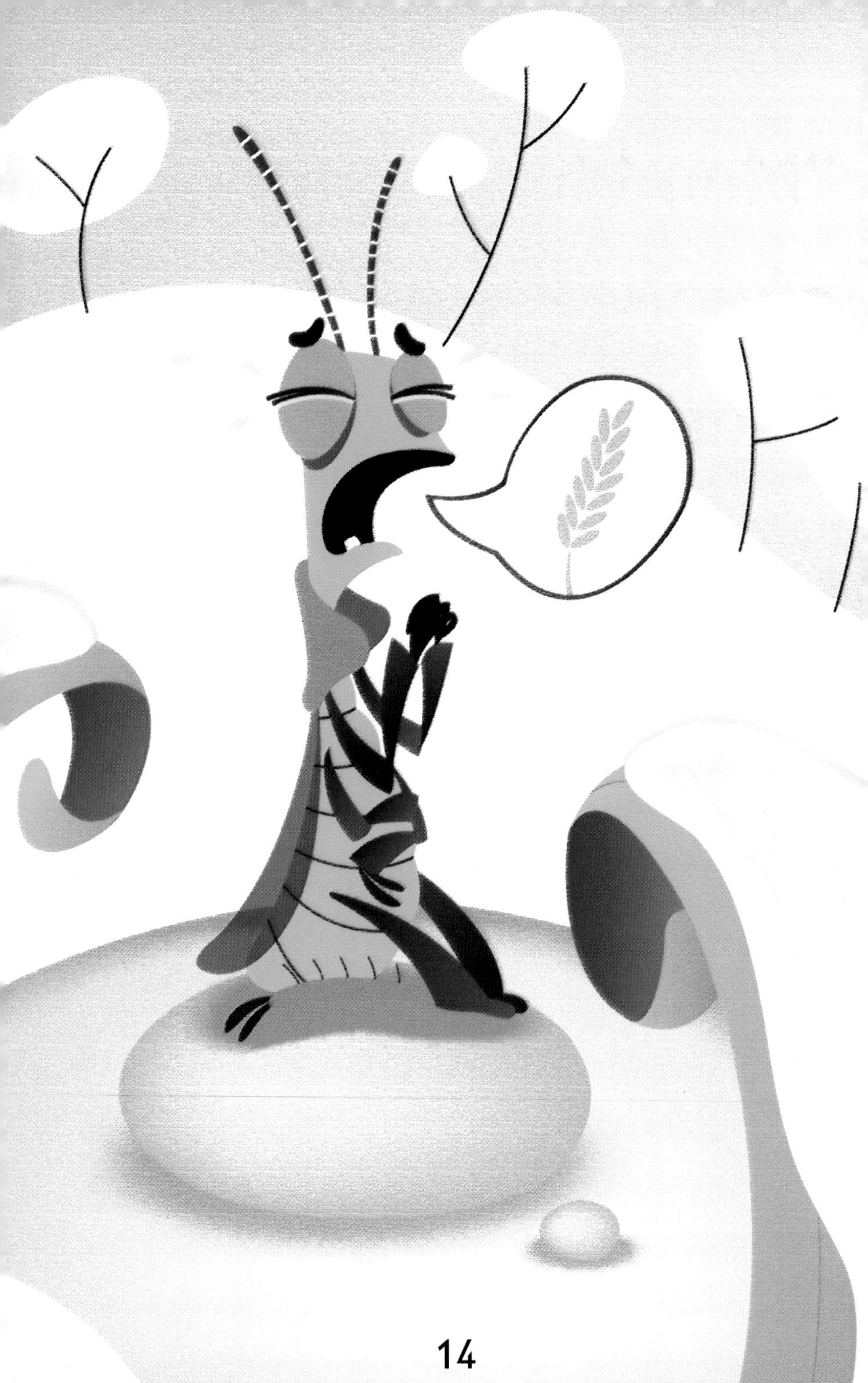

"May I have some of your grain?" Grasshopper asked.

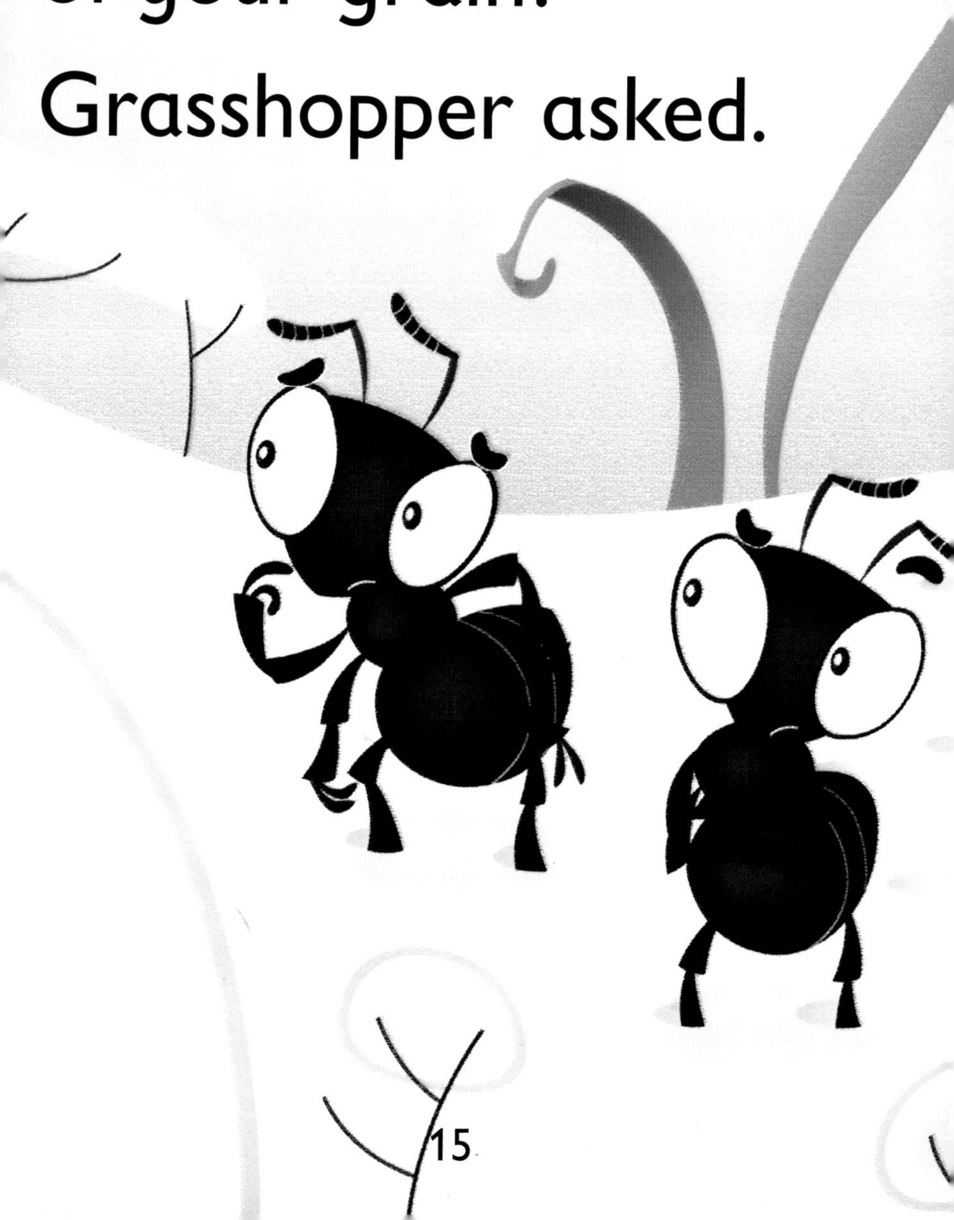

"Where is *your* grain?" Ant asked Grasshopper.

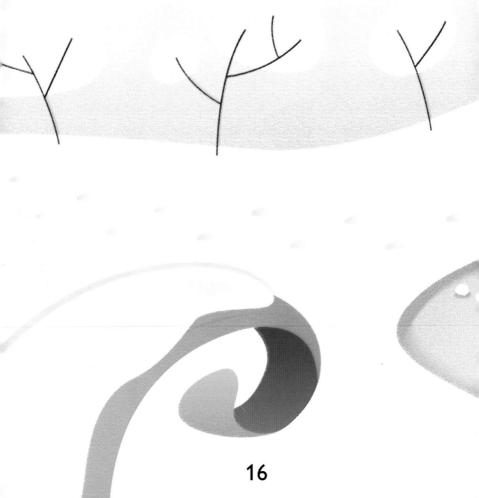

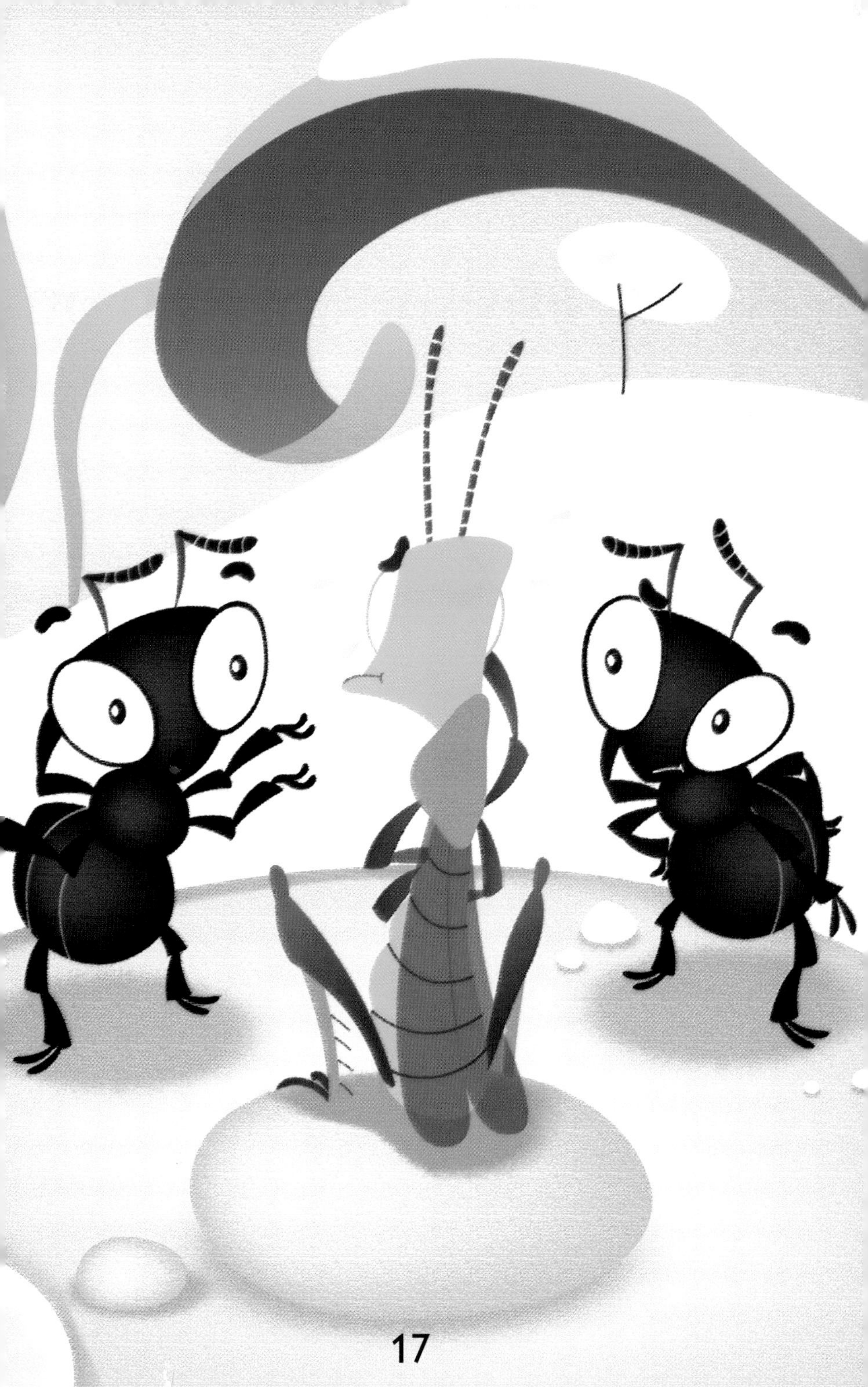

"I was too busy singing to go find any," said Grasshopper.

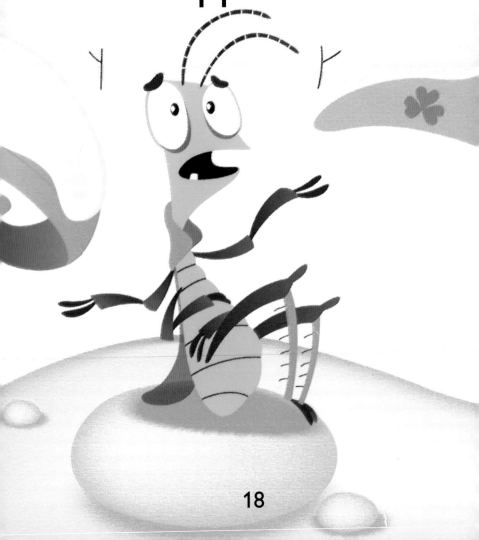

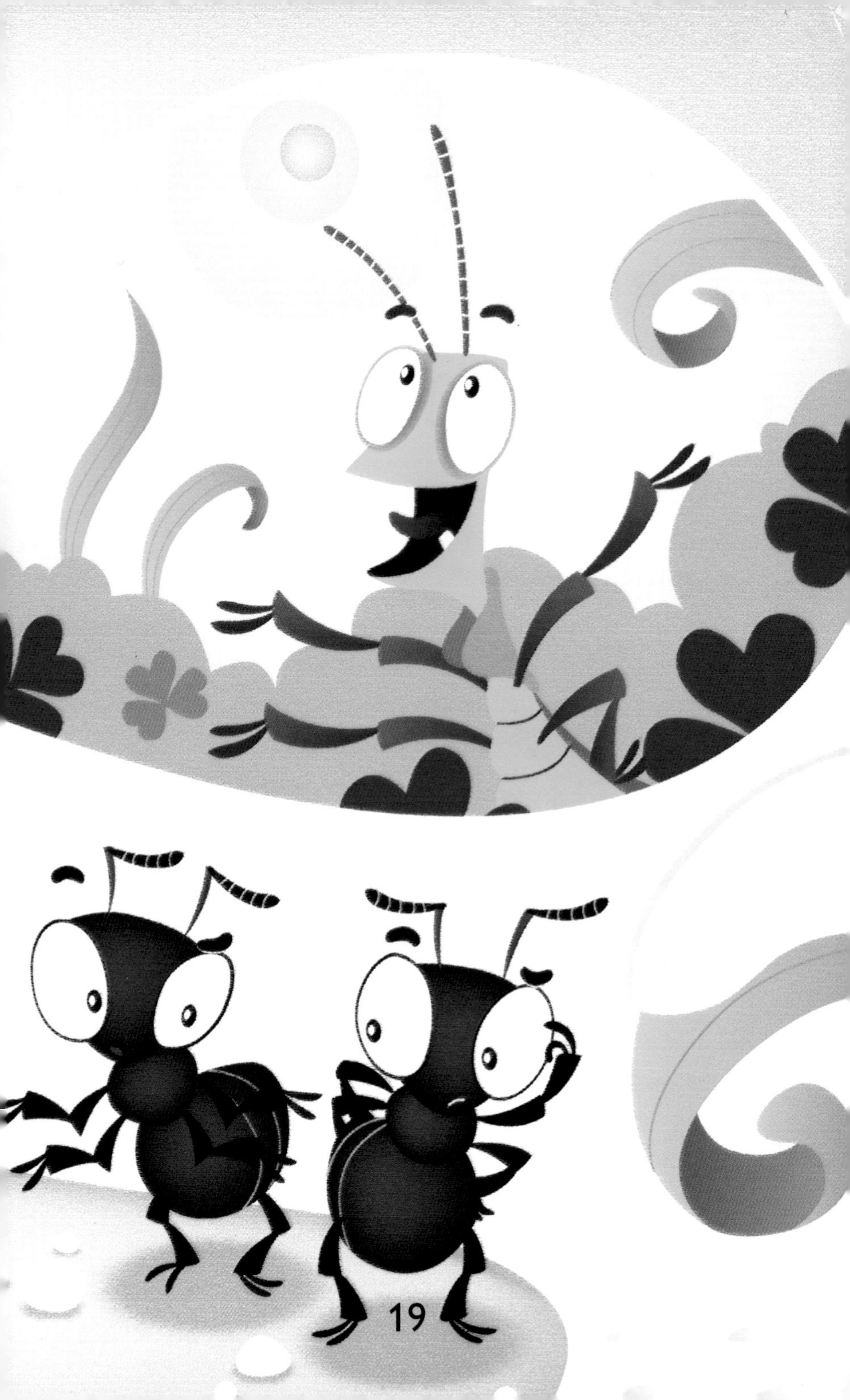

"You can have some grain, but next year you must find your own before winter," said Ant.

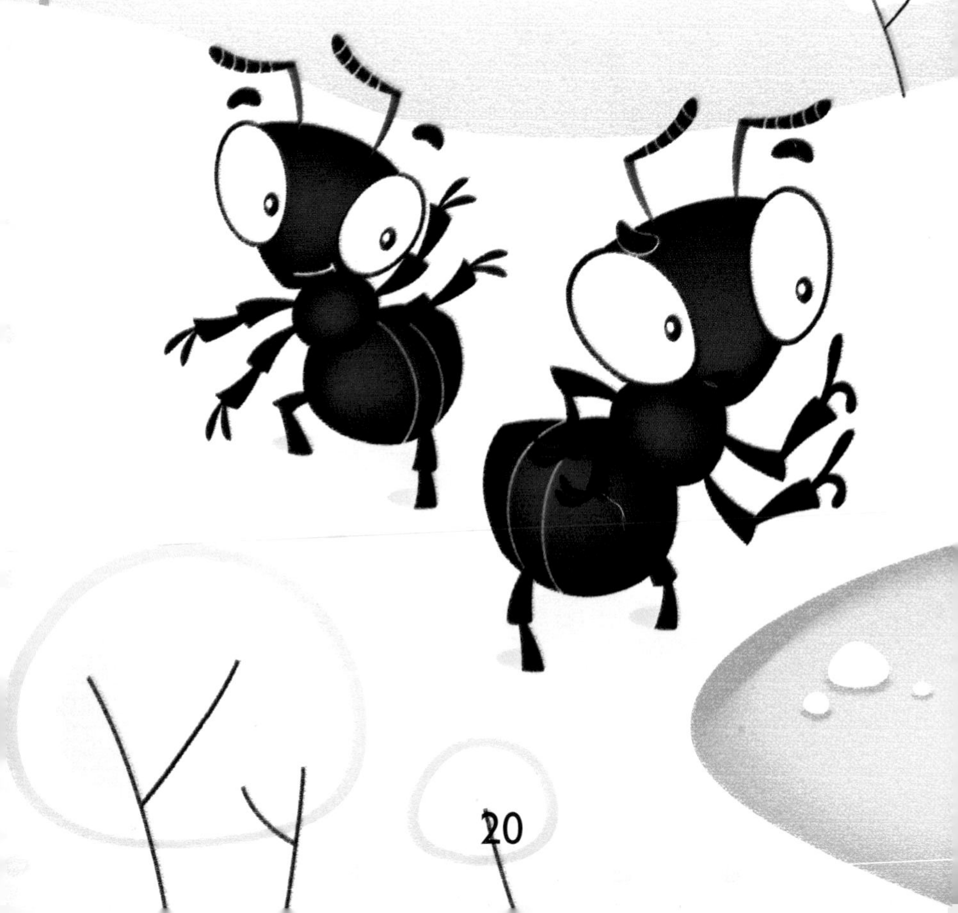

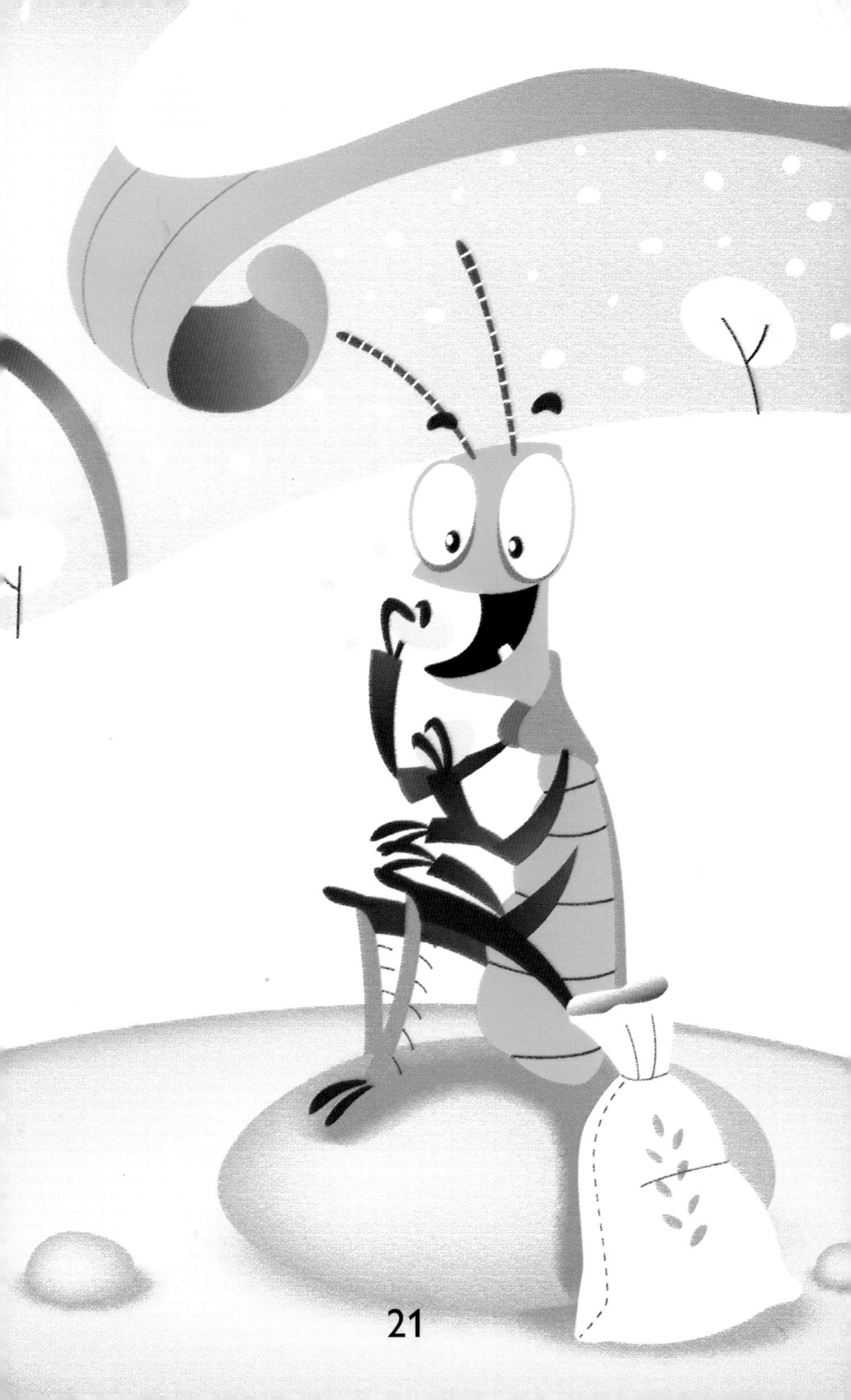

Puzzle Time!

a

b

c

d

e

f

Put these pictures in the right order and tell the story!

lazy

busy

idle

hardworking

Which words describe Ant and which describe Grasshopper?

Turn the page for the answers!

Notes for adults

TADPOLES: TALES are structured for emergent readers. The books may also be used for read-alouds or shared reading with young children.

The Ant and the Grasshopper is based on a classic fable by Aesop. Aesop's fables teach important principles about greed, patience, perseverance, and other character traits. Fables are a key type of literary text found in the Common Core State Standards.

IF YOU ARE READING THIS BOOK WITH A CHILD, HERE ARE A FEW SUGGESTIONS:

1. Make reading fun! Choose a time to read when you and the child are relaxed and have time to share the story.

2. Set a purpose for reading by explaining to the child that each of Aesop's fables teach a lesson. This information will help the reader understand the story and the features of the genre.

3. Encourage the child to reread the story and to retell it using his or her own words. Invite the child to use the illustrations as a guide.

4. Discuss the lesson of the story. Is the lesson important? Why or why not?

5. Give praise! Children learn best in a positive environment.

HERE ARE OTHER TITLES FROM TADPOLES: TALES FOR YOU TO ENJOY:

How the Camel got his Hump	978-0-7787-7888-2 RLB	978-0-7787-7900-1 PB
How the Elephant got its Trunk	978-0-7787-7891-2 RLB	978-0-7787-7903-2 PB
The Boy who cried Wolf	978-0-7787-7890-5 RLB	978-0-7787-7902-5 PB
The Fox and the Crow	978-0-7787-7892-9 RLB	978-0-7787-7904-9 PB
The Lion and the Mouse	978-0-7787-7893-6 RLB	978-0-7787-7905-6 PB

VISIT WWW.CRABTREEBOOKS.COM FOR OTHER CRABTREE BOOKS.

Answers

Here is the correct order!
1. a 2. b 3. d 4. f 5. c 6. e

Words to describe Ant:
busy, hardworking

Words to describe Grasshopper:
idle, lazy